# To Juniper, Long John, and Bronte-saurus

First edition 2015

Library of Congress Catalog Card Number 2013957318
ISBN 978-0-7636-6013-0

CCP 19 18 17 16 15
10 9 8 7 6 5 4 3 2

Printed in Shenzhen, Guangdong, China

This book was typeset in Aunt Mildred.
The illustrations were done in pencil and watercolor,
with some digital tweakery.

Candlewick Press
99 Dover Street
Somerville, Massachusetts 02144

visit us at www.candlewick.com

CANDLEWICK PRESS

# IF I HAD A
# TRICERATOPS

George O'Connor

If I had a triceratops,
I'd be sure to take good care of her.
Owning a triceratops is a lot of work.

I would give her a house of her own
in the backyard with lots of room
to run around.

(But I might let her sleep in my room when she gets scared.)

If I had a triceratops,

I would take her for lots and lots of walks.

(I'd be sure to clean up after her, of course.)

Going for walks would be a
great chance for my triceratops
to make new friends.

(And me too, I guess.)

Playing fetch would be another excellent way for her to get exercise.

If I had a triceratops,
I'd train her well and
teach her tricks,
like . . .

sit up,

roll over,

and play dead.

High Five!

I bet my triceratops would like to dig holes.

If she found any large bones,
I wouldn't let her chew on them.

She could choke.
(And besides, they might
belong to a relative of hers.)

When she gets dirty, I'll give her a bath.

If I had a triceratops, she would protect my home from burglars. (And maybe even the occasional T-Rex.)

And if sometimes she gets into trouble —
like for eating my homework . . .

or chasing the neighbor's car — well...

it will all be worth it

when she runs out to greet me

at the end of the day.

There's my girl!

If I had a triceratops,
I would be the luckiest kid in the world.